For Hester, with great love – G.E.
For Sasha – E.E.

little bee books

An imprint of Bonnier Publishing Group
853 Broadway, New York, NY 10003
Copyright © 2013 by Gareth Edwards.
Illustrations copyright© 2013 by Elina Ellis
First published in Great Britain by Piccadilly Press.
This little bee books edition, 2015.
LITTLE BEE BOOKS is a trademark of Bonnier Publishing Group,
and associated colophon is a trademark of Bonnier Publishing Group.
Manufactured in China 0215 024
First Edition 2 4 6 8 10 9 7 5 3 1
Library of Congress Control Number: 2014957614
ISBN 978-1-4998-0087-6

www.littlebeebooks.com
www.bonnierpublishing.com

The Littlest Bird

By Gareth Edwards

Illustrated by Elina Ellis

little bee books

There were seven green birds
in a beautiful nest
at the top of a tree
where the view was the best.

But the Littlest Bird
didn't like it at all,
for the beautiful nest
was incredibly small.

No place for her slippers,
her toothbrush and things—
and not even the space
to spread out her wings.

Her brothers and sisters
all borrowed her stuff,
and her mom didn't listen
or kiss her enough.

Every night when they tried
to sleep—what a squeeze!
What a wriggling tangle
of feathers and knees!

Every morning
the Littlest Bird really wished
that she didn't wake up
feeling jostled and squished.

So she said to herself,
"I am sick of this place.
They won't care if I move
to a nest with more space."

So she packed up her slippers,
her toothbrush and things,
and when no one was looking
she spread out her wings.

Then she fluttered about
over meadow and wood,
looking high, looking low
for a nest that was good.

But the nests that she found
didn't have enough space.
They were gloomy or drafty,
or in the wrong place.

Then on top of a mountain,
she stopped for a rest,
and she spotted a simply
INCREDIBLE nest!

It seemed to be empty
with no one in sight,
so she unpacked her things
and moved in for the night.

There was space for her slippers,
her toothbrush and things,
and whenever she liked
she could spread out her wings.

It was strange all the stillness
with no one around . . .

Then the Littlest Bird
heard a loud CRACKING
sound.

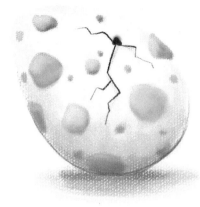

Through a hole
in an egg
poked a
short, scaly snout,

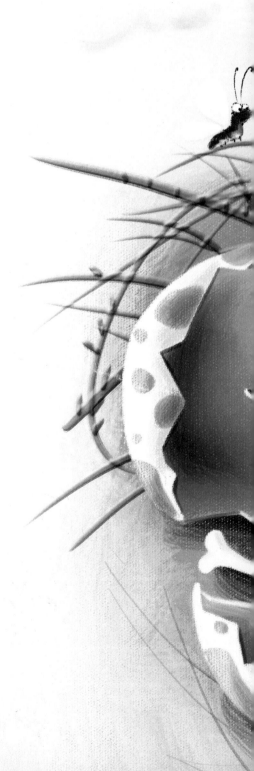

and the beady black eyes
of a dragon peeped out!

"Are you my mommy?"
the baby dragon said,
but the Littlest Bird
just shook her head.

Then she heard a voice calling,
"My baby, I'm here!"
and a big mother dragon
came hurrying near.

The Littlest Bird
watched them cuddle
each other.
She missed her own nest,
and she longed
for HER mother.

She looked at the dragons
and felt rather small.
She thought, "Maybe this place
isn't perfect at all."

She packed up her slippers,
her toothbrush and things.
She did not say goodbye,
she just spread out her wings.

Then she took to the air,
flying quick as could be,
and rushed back to her home
at the top of the tree.

Her mother said, "Darling!"
and cuddled and kissed her.
Her brothers and sisters
all said how they'd missed her.

With squishes and squeezes
and flurries of feather,
the birds and their mother
all huddled together.

And yes, it was crowded
and ever so small,
but the Littlest Bird
didn't mind that at all!